For Carla and Sandy Salteri,
who were the inspiration for Solos – D.B.

For Bruno – C.S.

Chapter 1

Carla didn't want much. She didn't want a bike. She didn't want a doll. She didn't even want chocolate spread for her lunch. What Carla wanted was gold rings in her ears.

"I want earrings!" she told her mother and father. But they said, "No."

"Little girls don't have rings in their ears," they said.

It made Carla mad, and it made her sad too. Nothing she said could make them change their minds.

Chapter 2

Rosa was Carla's best friend. They did everything the same. If Carla wore a green top, Rosa wore one too. If Rosa played on the monkey bars, Carla played there too.

Then one day, one thing wasn't the same. Rosa had little gold studs in her ears.

"You're so lucky," said Carla.

"Ask your mum and dad," said Rosa. "Then we can *both* have earrings!"

"No way." Carla looked down in
case she cried. "They won't let me."

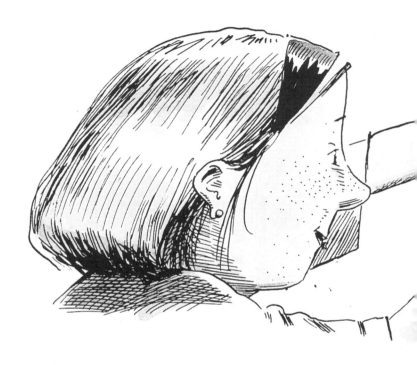

"Never mind," said Rosa. She
opened her pencil box. "We can
paint some on your ears."

She got out her gold felt-tip pen
and put little gold spots on Carla's
ears. But it wasn't the same.

"Mum," Carla said after school. "Rosa has earrings, and she's just a little girl like me. I want holes in my ears so I can put earrings in and out."

Carla's mother shook her head.

"I'm sorry," she said, and went on hanging out the washing. "No one in our family has ever had holes in their ears."

Carla frowned. Nothing was going
to change Mum's mind.

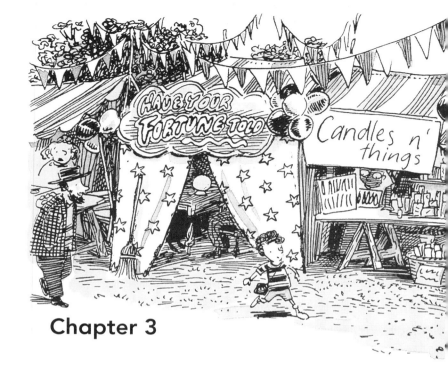

Chapter 3

Down the road was an old church, and every Saturday there was a big market there. Flags flew from red and blue tents. Balloons were tied up in big bunches with ribbons. You could buy pretty candles and silk hair bands.

15

16

Carla loved the market on Saturday.

While Mum and Dad had coffee and cake, she went for a walk.

Near the street there was a girl
selling paper flowers. In her nose
was a silver stud.

"That looks nice." Carla felt shy.

"Thanks," said the girl.

"But how do you blow your nose?" asked Carla.

The girl smiled. "Same as you do," she said.

"Can you take that stud in and out and turn it round?"

"You ask a lot of questions," said the girl.

"I'm sorry," said Carla. "It's just that I'd like a stud in my nose."

"You'll have to ask your mum," said the girl.

Mum was still drinking her coffee.

"The girl who sells paper flowers has a stud in her nose." Carla crossed her fingers. "I want a stud in my nose."

Carla's mum looked over the top of her cup and shook her head. "I'm sorry," she said. "No one in our family has a stud in their nose."

Carla felt like stamping her feet.

Chapter 4

In the afternoon they went to a
circus. The boy who sold popcorn
and drinks had a ring in his eyebrow.
It was blue, and a little bell hung
down from it. Each time he moved
his head, the little blue bell tinkled.

Carla wanted to ask if the bell got in his eyes, but she didn't in case it was rude. She wanted to ask how he washed his face. But she didn't.

"I'd like a ring in my eyebrow with
a little bell hanging off it," she said.

The boy smiled. "You'll have to
ask your dad," he said.

"Can I have a ring in my eyebrow with a little bell that tinkles?" she asked when she got back to her seat.

"I'm sorry," said Dad. "No one in our family has a ring in their eyebrow."

Carla felt like tipping her popcorn out all over the ground.

Chapter 5

Next Saturday morning they went to the beach. In the water Carla saw a lady with a ring in her belly button. It had a pretty green stone in the middle. When the lady stood up, the green stone looked like a little bit of wet seaweed that had got stuck there.

"That's a very nice ring in your tummy," said Carla, bobbing in the sea beside her. "I'd like a ring in my belly button like that."

"You had better ask your mum and dad then," said the lady, before she dived under the water.

"Mum? Dad?" Carla sat on the sand next to them. "Can I have a ring in my belly button with a green stone in it?"

Her mother and father didn't even look up from their books. "I'm sorry," they both said. "No one in our family has a ring in their belly button!"

They smiled at each other.

"It's not fair!" shouted Carla. "I can't have anything I want unless someone in my family has it too!"

She wouldn't speak to her mum
and dad for the rest of the day.

Chapter 6

On Sunday afternoon there was a
knock on the front door.

Carla went and opened it.

At the door stood a man with a
big bag in his hand.

"Hello," he said. "You must be Carla. I'm your mum's brother, Harry. We haven't met before. I've been living in America for ten years."

Carla stared at Uncle Harry. She had never seen anyone like him. He had long hair and a funny hat. And he had drawings all over him.

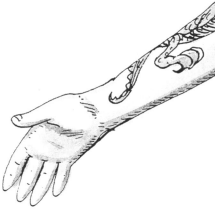

There was a dragon blowing fire
that went all the way up his arm.
There was a rose with the word
"Mother" above the petals, and a
very nice butterfly on his left hand.

43

"I like those pictures," she said.

"Thanks," said Uncle Harry. "They're called tattoos." He took off his hat and pushed back his hair.

Carla wanted to jump for joy. In Uncle Harry's ear was a gold ring.

"You're one of our family, aren't you?" she said.

"Why yes, I am," said Uncle Harry.

"Come in." Carla was looking very happy. "Mum and Dad will be *so* pleased to see you."

Dyan Blacklock

I wanted earrings when I was a little girl, but my mum always said *no*. I had to wait till I was grown up before I got holes in my ears – and *ouch!* They hurt!

Now I don't wear my earrings very often, but I see lots of girls and boys with rings in all kinds of funny places. I think it must hurt a lot to get a hole in your nose, or your belly button. It's more fun to have earrings when you are young, I think. I still wish my mum had let me have them!

Craig Smith

No one in my family ever had tattoos or rings in odd places, or funny hair styles. Now I am grown up and I can't even change my hair style because my hair has fallen out!

Not long ago I started to draw a dragon tattoo for myself (it was a silly dragon, not a scary one), but I couldn't decide where I wanted it to go. My daughter asked if she could have a small tattoo as well. As soon as I said yes, she lost interest. I wonder why?

More Solos!

Dog Star
Janeen Brian and Ann James

The Best Pet
Penny Matthews and Beth Norling

Fuzz the Famous Fly
Emily Rodda and Tom Jellett

Cat Chocolate
Kate Darling and Mitch Vane

Jade McKade
Jane Carroll and Virginia Barrett

I Want Earrings
Dyan Blacklock and Craig Smith

What a Mess Fang Fang
Sally Rippin

Cocky Colin
Richard Tulloch and Stephen Axelsen